Live Life Worthwhile

70 Ways to Enjoy it

Murli Chari

PUSTAK MAHAL®

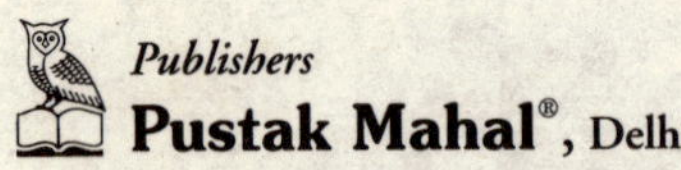

Publishers
Pustak Mahal®, Delhi

J-3/16 , Daryaganj, New Delhi-110002
☏ 23276539, 23272783, 23272784 • *Fax:* 011-23260518
E-mail: info@pustakmahal.com • *Website:* www.pustakmahal.com

Sales Centre

- 10-B, Netaji Subhash Marg, Daryaganj, New Delhi-110002
  ☏ 23268292, 23268293, 23279900 • *Fax:* 011-23280567
  E-mail: rapidexdelhi@indiatimes.com
- 6686, Khari Baoli, Delhi-110006
  ☏ 23944314, 23911979

Branches

Bengaluru: ☏ 080-22234025 • *Telefax:* 080-22240209
E-mail: pustak@airtelmail.in • pustak@sancharnet.in

Mumbai: ☏ 022-22010941, 022-22053387
E-mail: rapidex@bom5.vsnl.net.in

Patna: ☏ 0612-3294193 • *Telefax:* 0612-2302719
E-mail: rapidexptn@rediffmail.com

Hyderabad: *Telefax:* 040-24737290
E-mail: pustakmahalhyd@yahoo.co.in

ISBN 978-81-223-1357-4

Edition 2012

Printed at *:*Param Offsetters, Okhla, Delhi

Acknowledgements

I would like to thank all the authors who inspired me, our family friend Sumati Sanjay who endeavored to make the content free from semantic mistakes and irrelevant matters. I would like to place on record my gratitude to my wife Gheena, son Roshan and all my friends who helped me in making this book what it is today by providing suggestions.

Special thanks to the team at Pustak Mahal for having immense faith in my abilities as a writer.

Foreword

The book, Live Life Worthwhile is simple to read and easy to understand.

Each chapter speaks of leading a better life by practicing self-discipline, self-introspection, positive thinking and leading life in a simple manner with a clear conscience.

Each chapter ends with an anecdote which is a real life example to support the message.

The chapters are meant for easy reading and could be read individually from anywhere without having to read in a sequence.

The noteworthy point is that the book does not dwell into a theme which limits one in a particular confine. It's meant for easy and light reading for all age groups. I am sure after going through this enlightening work, one would be encouraged to lead a better quality of life.

Sumati Sanjay

School Coordinator

Pune

Contents

01

Be A Good Human-being; Contribute To The Society

As per Indian scriptures human life comes after Eighty Four Lacs Births

Human Beings are the Crowning Glory of All creations of Nature

– William Shakespeare

To be born as a human being is probably the most wonderful and miraculous gift. Years of evolution of mankind has made the man what he is today. It has been a tortuous route. One should not squander this wonderful gift on frivolous things and fritter away life on being jealous, greedy and hateful. Every one has a limited time span within which one has to do so many things and achieve one's dreams.

It is incomprehensible how people find time for criticizing, complaining and condemning when so very little time is there for self-improvement, excellence, creativity, love and human activities. One should try to devote one's time to achieve one's cherished dreams and contributing something worthwhile to the society. Don't waste time on useless activities like gossiping, criticizing, hating, back-biting and whiling away time.

Make the most of the limited time. You can earn back the lost money but time once lost is lost for ever. You can not turn the clock back. There are plethora of great people who have inhabited our world like Edison, Henry Ford, Mahatma Gandhi, Buddha, Socrates, Aristotle, Shakespeare, George Bernard Shaw, Mother Teresa, Benjamin Franklin and the like who have done so much that we should be inspired by them. One must have a worthy cause to devote one's life so that there are no boring moments. We will always be enthusiastic, energetic, euphoric and enduring, and you will like to treasure every moment of our life.

We must count our blessings and not what we do not have. In modern era we are blessed with so many beautiful things that we must be grateful to many people who due to their unstinted perseverance created those things. Imagine one day without electricity, fan, television, computers, automobiles, trains and a litany of things but for which our lives would not have been so beautiful, fantastic, gorgeous and wonderful.

Nature has been so bountiful without asking anything in return. It is the bounden duty of each one of us to contribute to society and nature. Presently we are busy destroying nature by polluting everything right from water, air, ecology. There is an urgent need to restore ecology back to its virgin status. If everyone does his best towards nature, we will have virtually created heaven on earth. We should emulate the greats who made this world a better place and not emulate anti-social, criminals and derelicts who have made this world a bitter place.

We are so embroiled in our mundane activities that we have forgotten the rich heritage we have inherited from the earlier generations. We are fast exhausting the resources of nature that we will not be able to treasure the rich gifts of nature for posterity.

This is a colossal abuse of what we have been handed over by earlier generations. The earth collectively belongs to everyone and individually to none. We should put an end to nuclear proliferation at the earliest since there are so many disgruntled and sadist people who would not mind to use the nuclear option. The nuclear devastation will permanently damage the flora and fauna and the delicate balance of ecology. Do we have the right to do this? As Gandhiji said, a need can be satisfied but not greed. We must restrain the unbridled exploitation of nature.

We must create a Third Wave civilization on a sustainable growth and stop using fossil fuels as envisioned by Alvin Toffler in his book *Third Wave*. We must all make conscious efforts to restore sanity to the disturbed world. We must all coalesce the energy and efforts of all towards a common goal. We must not be self-centered in all our activities. We must spare some time towards making this world free of poverty, ignorance and oligarchy.

Human-beings are very different from other animals. We must count ourselves fortunate to have been born as human beings. Let us pledge that all of us will work towards a common goal of paradise on earth.

Anecdote

As per Hindu mythology once a Rakshasha named Bhasmasur prayed for a long time to God Shiva who was very much pleased to grant him any boon. The evil man that Bhasmasur was, he asked for the boon that any person/animal on whose head he places his hand will turn into bhasma i.e. ashes.

Bhasmasur got the boon and wanted to try his trick on God Shiva. He tried to place his hand on God Shiva's head

but God Shiva ran helter-skelter and prayed to Lord Vishnu to save him. Lord Vishnu took the disguise of a beautiful damsel Mohini and stood before the rakshasa.

Bhasmasura was very much tempted and proposed to Mohini for marriage. Mohini said she would marry if Bhasmasura agreed to her conditions to do whatever she does.

Mohini started dancing and Bhasmasura also started dancing and copying whatever Mohini did. Ultimately Mohini placed her hand on her head and Bhasmasura also placed his hand on his head and was immediately turned into ash.

To apply the same analogy to today's life, a person who tries to destroy the world will also meet the same fate of Bhasmasura. A person living by sword shall also die of sword.

02

Character Is The Foundation

Vinasha Kalaye Viprita Buddhi

(When bad times come your mind goes berserk)

A human life without character is a body without soul. Character is a sum total of many virtues or vices. However much the society advances the character is the foundation for a society to survive. We must have faith, honesty, integrity, sincerity and love for all.

A person without character may have achieved success but his life is meaningless unless he has character. A rich person without character may not enjoy respect and reputation from the society. Whereas a poor man with character will command a lot of respect. Characterless person one day meets his nemesis.

A person with character may not have the riches rather he may find the going tough but he is a happy man because he is at peace with himself. He has no fear of getting caught doing the wrong things. He has a clear and a vibrant conscience. He does not have to put up with sleepless nights. He will have no reason to hide his face and can combat any situation without resorting to unethical things. There is an old saying as under which is priceless and worth the need to be part of one's life :

When wealth is lost , nothing is lost.

When health is lost something is lost.

When character is lost everything is lost.

From this, it is clear that character is the most important thing in life. Tall buildings are built on strong foundation and can withstand any onslaught without difficulty. If you want to stand tall then have character as your foundation.

A person's character is known at the time of adversity. A rich man can afford to be ethical. But it requires character for a man with small resources. Only the life's critical moments calls for character to withstand the crisis. A characterless person will fall prey to any temptation and get into the vicious circle of evil. He gets into the muddle of evil acts that ultimately leads him astray and gets him into abysmal depths. He gets stuck in the quagmire that he cannot pull himself out.

A person with a character on the contrary faces all the problems sportively and comes out unscathed. Never ever leave the support of character even under the most trying situations. It is the way of the world to test a person of character and ultimately he gets rewarded for his strength of character. Characterless people enjoy success for a short period of time but vanish into thin air when they get exposed.

Be a person with character and feel the pleasure. To sum up, character is best described as under :

Character leads to Courage

Courage leads to Confidence

Confidence leads to Commitment

Commitment leads to Completion

Completion leads to Celebration.

Anecdote

Everyone knows the story of Harshad Mehta. He started as a modest typist in the investment department of The New India Assurance Co. Ltd. at Mumbai. He learned the tricks of Stock Market at Dalal Street, just behind the Head Office of New India Assurance Co. Ltd. He sold his typewriter and ventured into the stock market and rose mercurially and became the cynosure of all investing public including the docile middle class, which came in droves to the market like bees to nectar.

He walked like a colossus endearing himself to all and sundry and made share market a bull's paradise. Everyone was making a fortune. Then suddenly the bubble burst and many people lost their shirts. It dawned on everyone that he fabricated and rigged the prices and took everyone for a ride. He conned everyone. Many people lost their life's savings , banks lost crores and financial institutions lost millions.

Harshad Mehta amassed a lot of wealth by resorting to unethical and devious means. He was living a lavish life at the cost of others. He was put behind the bars and when he died there was none to commiserate.

Such is the quirk of fate; you are king one day and gone the other day.

••

Be A Good Citizen

> Do unto others what you expect others to do to you

Man is a social animal.

We are part of the society and need to give and receive in return from the society. We can not live in isolation. To consider oneself above all is height of superciliousness. But for society we would still be roaming in the jungles with very meagre progress.

Civilization was possible due to the existence of society. Therefore it is the bounden duty of all to follow the rules and regulations framed by the society. We have rights as well as duties. True rights arise from duties only.

Of late it has become ubiquitous to find everyone hankering after rights forgetting the duties are the other side of the same coin. There are glaring, blatant examples of flouting the rules for one's own benefit without realizing how it affects others and how it vitiates civilized living. We do not have the patience to stand in the queue, waiting in the traffic signals. We are always looking for shortcuts to everything including achieving one's goals. We Indians have blatant disregard for cleanliness in public places.

However, we are meticulous when it concerns our homes. We have no hesitation in bribing to get even the straight and simple things done. Being honest by yourself is not sufficient. We need to exercise restrain whenever the situation arises to grease the palms.

Generations of the earlier periods have persevered and made a lot of sacrifices to make this world a better place to live. We also need to contribute our mite to the society to express our gratitude to the people who have made worthwhile contribution to human society.

All our education is a waste if we only make demands to the society and do nothing in return. We owe so much to the society that however much we do is very little. If everyone of us makes a contribution in proportion to one's capacity we can fulfill our most exotic dreams. If we have the wisdom, knowledge, education and resources then we must not flinch from doing the best and taking up the leadership and responsibility. Society beckons such people as they are very rare to find. Being a good citizen means we should be free from all biases of religion, caste, creed, race, country. We need to have patience and tolerance.

As one saying goes :

God give me the courage to change the things I can

The serenity to accept the things I cannot and

The wisdom to know the difference.

Don't wait for others to do what you know and can do. You need to take up the leadership. You will have enough pleasure in doing good to others. Miracles can happen if only you dream, dare and do. Everything in this world has been invented, discovered and done by ordinary people with extraordinary dreams. Light a lamp instead of complaining. Seize the initiative and do your best, then others will follow you automatically. You are endowed with unlimited potential but are stuck in a state of inertia. Even a small beginning ends up in colossus. Each step in the right direction will take you to your destiny. Pursuing personal ambitions should be in harmony with the good of others. There are people in this world who will discourage, criticize and ridicule you but don't vacillate from your cherished dream of bringing sanity to the world.

Anecdote

There are many examples in this world for us to emulate that we should not complain.

Shaheed Bhagat Singh laid down his life seeking independence for India at the tender age of 23.

George Washington and others took the extreme step to seek freedom from the mighty British Empire.

Thomas Edison hardly went to school but his achievements are abundant.

So we cannot take the excuse of lack of education, money and time. We are fortunate to have all the infrastructure to do our best.

Our own legend Chatrapati Shivaji showed so much of courage to fight the Moguls instead of caring for his life, family and fortune.

Of late Annasaheb Hazare is doing everything to bring clean governance and transparency the people of India.

Mother Teresa attended to the destitute without caring for her personal comforts. Soldiers lay down their lives for the sake of civilian people.

The list of people who silently work for the welfare of the society is endless.

••

04

Be Free From Biases

> Beauty is skin deep — *William Shakespeare*

Our thinking has been so shaped by the pseudo leaders, both political and religious, that we hate and are biased against people of other castes, religions, countries and regions.

Religious bias has probably killed more people than diseases and natural calamities. With the onset of knowledge and tremendous technological advancement the whole world is becoming a global village. We must shed our biases based on frivolous things in order to develop healthy relationships and bring literacy, prosperity and better understanding to the teeming millions. We should not have biases within our reach to make this world a better place.

Biases germinate from economic concerns. Knowledge based society has immense potential for true democracy and prosperity to all. Even in individual life we are unduly biased about others as it emanates from a sense of insecurity. Unbiased character permits to understand other people better, improving both communication and relationships.

All the people enjoy the same heritage, nature, ecology and environment. We are made of the same fabric by nature. Nature is a cornucopia to be enjoyed by all. Removing biases puts you on the threshold of greatness. Once a sufi saint/author Khalil Gibran said that anyone can be free without being great but no one can be great without being free. Why create artificial barriers as we are the favoured children of nature?

Do away with biases and achieve your potential to your own advantage and that of humanity. Bias is one of the cardinal issue that is responsible for the genocides, wars and terrorism apart from economic reasons. Years of biases cannot be done away with easily but we can make a move in that direction as it can make our lives worthwhile. Be bold and be unbiased, as boldness has genius, magic and power.

Anecdote

India could have been a great country as it has a rich heritage and tradition. Religious bias of Hindus and Muslims has been the raison daitre for partition. Precious human lives were lost at the time of partition because of religious bias leading to needless acrimony between the two countries.

Racial bias was the cause of II nd World War. Apartheism in South Africa was the classic example of racial bias.

In India we have the communal, caste and linguistic bias that it is proving to be our unbecoming. Going from one state to another state gives one the impression that one is traveling in an alien country.

••

05

Be A Good Listener

> Nature has provided you with two ears and one mouth as you should listen twice as much as you speak.

Being a good listener requires lot of patience, tolerance, concentration, focus and understanding. But this virtue can provide you astounding rewards. Even nature has given us two ears and one mouth so that we listen twice as much as we talk.

Being a good listener makes you a great communicator and a friend. Allowing others to have their say gives the other person a great joy and he regards you as a good person. If both are competing with each other to speak, it leads to argument and communication gap notwithstanding lack of social manners and etiquettes. Good listening increases your knowledge, wisdom and broadens one's horizon as everyone has something worthwhile to share.

Anecdote

Children and students learn and understand everything by listening intently. In sales also if one does not listen carefully one may undersell or wrong sell. Listening with full focus is necessary to lessen the communication gap. Listening enables absorption of knowledge. Listening without focus will make your mind wander. The legendary Arjun, the ace archer was an intent listener. He listened to his coach Dronacharya intently and learnt archery and became a champion. He listened to his best friend and mentor Lord Krishna and learnt the great poetic gospel Bhagwat Gita.

••

06

Always Side Justice

Sun shines equally on King and the subjects

It is one of the greatest challenges to be on the side of justice. Mostly we side with the high and mighty for fear of recrimination. However, you must have the courage to support justice though it may require you to take side with the weak and the meek.

You must listen to the dictates of your conscience as that will make you strong and you will be trusted and admired by one and all. In the long run, you will feel proud and elated about your stand. By siding justice you will be secured of support in case you become a victim of injustice yourself. In the short run, you will be put to an acid test but if you have the resolve then you will come out with flying colours.

By siding with justice the kind of peace you enjoy cannot be measured in terms of material rewards but spiritually and emotionally you will enjoy sublime happiness. In these days of blatant opportunism it is very tough to be on the side of justice. But if you practice to be on the side of justice you will have made many friends and earned lot of praise. You will become an oasis of virtue in the desert of rank opportunism.

In United Kingdom years ago Prime Minister Tony Blair's son was arrested for drunken brawl. That speaks volumes about the system of justice prevailing there.

Justice is said to be blind and acts without having any regard to one's financial or social position. But in reality this is very rare. The poor, weak and the underprivileged of the society bear the brunt of injustice.

No doubt, it is a tall order to side the justice. Whoever raises the issue of justice is silenced and mocked. But it is the cardinal requirement of a free society. Everyone has to make a small sacrifice to make the society a better institution. Justice delayed is justice denied. Give it an honest try and you will derive great satisfaction.

Anecdote

Once upon a time in ancient India a king had installed a big bell at the entrance of his palace for people to seek king's justice. Once a cow started ringing the bell and everyone was astonished at this gesture.

King came out and found that a cow was ringing the bell. A big mob was following the cow and met the king and told that cow was seeking justice for its offspring which was marauded by a chariot. King immediately ordered the person to be flogged.

The mob requested the king to withhold his orders as the person responsible for the death of the calf was none other than king's son.

The king refused to withdraw his fiat and asked to carryout his orders. The king's men started flogging the prince. But the mob prayed to god and asked for forgiveness.

Ultimately the gods were pleased and revived the calf and also saved king's son for they were very much impressed by the king's gesture of giving justice without partiality.

In present days we have two standards; one for ourselves and one for others. One more instance from the great Hindu epic Ramayana is worth mentioning.

When Lord Rama returned from Lanka after vanquishing the demon king Ravana he had to face the stark reality of putting Sita, his console, to the test of fire. He could have as well avoided. Sita sacrificed herself to prove her chastity. Lord Rama is considered as the epitome of virtues.

It takes a lot of courage to take the side of justice but the amount of praise you receive is beyond words.

••

07

Listen To Your Conscience

Your conscience knows your deeds, good or bad

Conscience is the god within you which knows everything you do, whether right or wrong. Listening to your conscience will always guide you in the right direction. Listening to the dictates is, no doubt, tough but it will never betray you if you listen to it. An active conscience is a boon. A clear conscience is one of the greatest boons that will stand you in crisis. A clear conscience gives you sound sleep. You can not hide anything from your conscience as it is an integral part of your personality. Make conscience your trusted ally come what may.

Never go against your conscience as that would in no time make you unscrupulous. If you vitiate your conscience at every occasion then you will have lost your best friend. All the great people in all the bygone days have always listened and acted as per conscience. Nourish your conscience everyday, every moment of your life. Discover the God by discovering your conscience. A good conscience is one of the prerequisite to becoming great.

Anecdote

We all know how Antulay lost his Chief Ministership as Justice Lentin listened to his conscience. He could well have collected the bounty and given a favourable justice to Antulay.

Dr. Nelson Mandela listened to his conscience and remained in the jail and ultimately his stand was vindicated when he won freedom from apartheid policies of the white. Just imagine the fate of the blacks had Nelson Mandela compromised with the whites for his personal freedom and fortune.

08

Acquire Knowledge From All Sources And Make Full Use Of It

Let Noble Thoughts come all over the Universe – Rig Veda

Knowledge is power. There is no dispute about it. Knowledge can reach even the darkest area where even sunlight doesn't reach. It is more formidable than the universe itself. A king's domain is his own kingdom whereas a knowledgeable person's domain is throughout the world.

Knowledge can be acquired from infinite sources. Knowledge can be found in books, scriptures, radio, television, CDs, internet, films, people, nature, universe, environment, and other sources. Even an illiterate person may possess a wealth of knowledge.

In the quest of knowledge, be modest as that will permit you to learn more and more. What you already know is only handful and what you have to know is the whole world. One life time is not enough to acquire all the knowledge that has accumulated in the world.

The day you feel you have learnt everything, that is the nadir of your ignorance. Potential of knowledge is unfathomable.

More important is to put to use whatever knowledge you have acquired for your and others' benefit. Of late knowledge has become most powerful, sending muscle and money power to oblivion. Any amount of money spent on acquiring true knowledge will not go waste as it would give you immense rewards in return. Acquiring knowledge and then disseminating it among others is the very purpose of pursuit of knowledge.

Knowledge and arrogance do not go together. The more you acquire, the more modest you should become. Knowledge if shared amongst all will make this world a better place to live in. Knowledge must not be used for purely material gains. Don't confine pursuit of knowledge to a particular subject. First and the foremost priority should be to acquire knowledge to make you a better person and truly mature and complete in all respects. Merely gathering information, cramming and filling your mind will be of no use. Remove the incorrect facts from information and turn it into knowledge. Knowledge will make you modest, rich, famous, charismatic and confident.

Anecdote

The classic examples of knowledge bringing you rich rewards are so many.

Bill Gates using his knowledge became the richest person in the world. Our own Narayan Murthy has risen from an ordinary man to build a mighty empire of Infosys. Sabeer Bhatia made millions by creating Hotmail. J.K.Rowling, the writer of Harry Potter-series of books is richer than Queen Elizabeth of Great Britain. There are many rags to riches stories who have made use of knowledge and became rich.

Of late more than money, knowledge has become the capital to reap rich rewards. One idea is enough to make you rich, famous and free.

The great saints of yester years spread knowledge for the benefit of the people in general and not for their personal gains.

The mighty king of Lanka, Ravana had the knowledge of ten heads but his arrogance became his reason of downfall.

To keep knowledge a secret is one of the greatest sins. If you know something you should share it with others. Knowledge spent increases the treasure of knowledge unlike money which once spent is lost.

••

09

Always Be Positive

> One person was moaning that he had no shoes
> until he saw a person without a foot

Being positive always pays. Looking at positive things in life saves you a lot of worries. Looking at negative things in life makes you cynical, gloomy and leaves bitter taste in the mouth. When your outlook is negative you will always have reason to complain, criticize and condemn. Positive attitude can be best described as under:

Always look to the

positive things in life

like a Sunflower

which always faces

the Sun.

Getting into the negative frame of mind makes you fall in a vicious circle and will never permit you to look things in proper perspective. A negative person will look at the black spots in the beautiful moon. In this world there are both positive and negative things. Once you start looking to the negative side you will find a lot to ridicule. On the other hand there are a lot of positive things in the world which will make you cheerful and enthusiastic.

In the same way if you look to the negative side of a person you will despise him and will never focus on his good qualities though they may be in plenty.

For a healthy and pleasant relation always focus on the positive side of everything and everyone. By doing this you will always be cheerful and happy. Make it a point to catch people doing the right things and appreciate it and not the other way round.

The die-hard critics will always criticize the weather, people and things. There are so many reasons like the bountiful nature, a child's smile etc to be happy about.

There is a common attitude of complaining about nature. Be it summer, be it winter or be it monsoon. Every season has its own role to play in nature to support life on earth. Summer, monsoon and the winter, the eternal trinity makes life beautiful on earth.

So if you look at things from the positive angle you will find good reasons to carry on life with enthusiasm. By being positive you will relish every moment of your life. Human life is so wonderful, gorgeous and beautiful that you must thank God or nature for that and look at the positive things in life to make your life a wonderful experience rather than being depressed and disappointed.

Anecdote

Thomas Edison was deaf and hardly went to school for three months. But he always looked at the positive things in life. His deafness worked to his advantage as he did not have to hear words of discouragement and criticism. Once his laboratory was burned to ashes.

Any other person would have lamented and cursed his fate but Edison thanked god that all his faults were burnt. He tried 10000 trials and experiments before inventing the electric bulb.

Dr. Nelson Mandela always remained positive when he was in prison for 27 years. The great Abraham Lincoln retained his positive attitude inspite of all the early failures.

••

10

Dream Big Dreams and Give Your Best to Fulfill Them

> A dream without action is useless
> and an action without dream is a nightmare

Dream is one of the rarest quality that is unique to human-beings.

Dreams while asleep is a body mechanism to flush trash from our minds. Whereas dreaming while awake is one which makes us work towards a goal. Everything in the world which was created had its genesis in a dream. Nothing can be achieved without a dream in life.

Plant a seed in your mind and nourish it regularly to help it grow and take roots. Beautiful edifices, monuments, paintings, sculptures, work of art, everything started with a dream. Aim for the stars and even if you do not succeed you will have achieved something worthwhile.

Write down your dreams in a notebook and feed them into your subconscious. Keep your cherished dreams to yourself till you are confident of fulfilling them.

People, friends, relatives and your near and dear ones will criticize and discourage you. Be honest to yourself and never let your dream be replaced by regrets. With regular nourishment and care, your dream seed will grow into a big tree bearing fruits, giving shade and comfort. Take up the challenge and do your best. Plan, persevere and be patient while treading the unknown path.

The world honours those who fulfill their dreams. Your fantastic dreams have a chance to survive if you provide succor, imagination and make result-oriented efforts. Human life without a dream is equivalent to a barren land. Differentiate between dreams and wishful thinking. Blend your dreams with enthusiasm, belief, confidence and diligence at that end.

Anecdote

Walt Disney achieved the impossible. When he made the cartoons of Mickey mouse and Donald Duck he was ridiculed and made a butt of laughter. However, he had faith in his dreams and now the rest is history.

Kroc of the famous MacDonald's had only $ 20 and was lying on a bench when he dreamt of MacDonald's chain of hotels.

Stretch your dreams to the extreme. Henry Ford dreamt of building an 8 cylinder engine for his car. His belief in his dreams paid rich dividends. Our own Late Dhirubhai Ambani while working as an attendent at a petrol pump, dreamt of owning an oil company. He did realize his dream.

It is not the size of the dream which is daunting but your own belief.

11

Be a Role Model

> Be always a trail blazer to become a role model

Being a role model fills the vacuum in the world to be emulated by others. There is a great dearth of role models in the world. Younger generations are devoid of role models to follow.

A person has so many roles to play in his life. You may be a son or a daughter, father or mother, husband or wife, employer or employee, customer or service-provider, member of a club and more. One has to blend various roles effectively to provide a role model for others.

As an offspring one has duties towards one's parents. Do everything to show your gratitude to your parents and elders. Be faithful to your friends. Be a faithful spouse. Be a good parent and set examples for your children to follow. One has to be a good citizen and contribute to the welfare of the society.

Educate both younger and older generations to adapt to changes in lifestyle. As a spouse share all the things in life and do everything to keep the relation sound. Never be a chauvinist. Be free from prejudices.

Don't treat your job as a commercial contract, always waiting to take advantage. Treat your job as an opportunity to help other people by solving their problems. Be loyal to your employer and do more than you receive. Sooner the rewards will come your way. Share your joy, worries, happiness and riches with everyone who is dear to you. Sympathize with the unfortunate and underprivileged. Empathize with others in their times of crisis.

As an employer do everything to keep your employees satisfied and give them a sense of belonging to the organization. Be generous, helpful and friendly to all. Be a paragon of virtue and be a good role model in every aspect of your life.

Expect the best from life and you will receive it. If you settle for less, then the world will give you only that much. The joy of being a role model in all frontiers is beyond words. A role model is respected, rewarded and honoured by the society. If you take up the challenge you will grow in your esteem and in the eyes of world. There is a great opportunity beckoning you to fill the role of a role model in present times. Role models do something different and do the trail blazing. You have to be unconventional in your approach.

Anecdote

Gandhiji became the role model during the struggle for independence of India. People flocked to him like bees to honey. Narayanmurthy, Azim Premji of India and Bill Gates are the kind of role models younger generations are looking for.

Do Good To Others And Get The Best In Return

> When you are good to others you are best to yourself – Saint Thomas

Once a great saint said "When you are good to others you are best to yourself." It is our common experience to derive immense pleasure when we do good to others without expecting anything in return. You become ecstatic and feel out of the world.

When you do good just do it and forget. The same person may not reward you but someone will do good to you. It is a morale boosting experience and elevates your spirit when you help a perfect stranger. Doing good without expectations is an exhilarating and exciting experience which cannot be expressed in words. Doing good to others makes both the persons blissful. Doing good to others is good for your mental, emotional, physical and spiritual health. Do good no matter what others think.

Cynics have been there since time immemorial. If everyone does good we can turn this world into a heaven. There are no short-term gains but in the long run you will certainly be rewarded.

Dispel the darkness to some extent instead of complaining about darkness. Seize the initiative and persistently continue to do good.

Society has always been like this for eons and in that it has been unfair to many. This did not halt the force of do-gooders. Be a torch-bearer and trend-setter in doing good. We must accept the challenges society throws at us. If you persistently do good to others that will leave you little time to fret about your problems. In the ultimate analysis you get in return what you have given to the society. You reap what you sow. Natural forces also help you when you do good to others.

Human beings are the crowning glory of nature's creations. If you want to make your life momentous then look beyond yourself. That is the discerning difference between man and other animals. Man is endowed with the tremendous capacity both mental and physical to change this world beyond recognition. It is the essence of all religions.

Anecdote

As per Hindu mythology, in Ramayana Lord Rama sacrificed his throne at the behest of his step-mother and roamed in the dangerous forests for 14 years. But after the exile he returned to an overwhelming reception. He set an example for others to follow.

Gandhiji sacrificed everything for the sake of the country.

Netaji Subhashchandra Bose laid down his prestigious post of ICS and fought for the freedom of India.

••

13

Do Smart Work And Not Just Donkey(Hard) Work

> Akal Badi ki Bhais (Brain is bigger than buffalo)

Horses have neck and shoulder above donkeys. The reasons are quite obvious. Horse does smart work and donkeys carry the load. With due respect to donkeys they are considered inferior to horses as they are useful only for carrying load day in and day out. Donkeys work very hard but still horses get all the bouquets and donkeys get the brickbats.

Brains are better than muscles. Brains create incredible things whereas muscles create ordinary things. A man with a brain always walks away with rewards both material and spiritual. The most glaring difference between animals and man is his superior and highly developed brain. Hard work pays gradually. Smart work always pays. Even a cursory glance at the lifestyles enjoyed by hard-working and smart-working people will reveal who is more successful.

All the magnificient things we see in the world has been the brain-child of smart people. If you want to elevate the underprivileged and the poor then they need to be educated about the enormous advantages of smart work. There is so much of knowledge and wisdom available that anyone can make a paradigm shift in his style of working. Working smart helps both others and yourself. Smart work involves using all the faculties of your mind. Use your skill, imagination, creativity and knowledge to do your work. Thinking afresh about your work will make you smart.

Plan your work and work your plan. Read books on self-improvement. Always analyze your work and find shortcuts to do it faster and smarter. You have better chances of succeeding in your mission in life if you work smart. Work hard and work smart and fulfill all your goals. Discard your mental blockage and realize your full potential, for human life comes once. Make the most of your life and enjoy everything you desire and deserve. Destiny is beckoning you and the world is eagerly awaiting your arrival. The day you decide to work smart you have taken your own destiny in your hands.

Anecdote

Bill Gates is today one of the richest man. He became rich not just due to hard-work but due to smart work. He has made using the computers within reach of the ordinary people. His smartness has made others smart.

A person was working for 20 years cutting the trees. But he hardly made any money and struggled for existence. Then came another man who cut more trees than the former. The old worker was constantly reprimanded and praises were showered on the new man. Atlast the former employee contacted the new employee and asked him the reasons for his success. The new employee told him the secret. He sharpened his axe for half-a-day and then started cutting the trees. This is smart work.

Have Faith in Humanity

> It is better to believe and be cheated than not to believe at all

In these days of chaos, confusion, deceit, violence, crime, dishonesty, corruption and insensitiveness it is a tall order to expect people to have faith in humanity. Even in spite of all the things in turmoil and disorder it is very important to have faith in humanity as there are so many redeeming things in the world.

It is only the handful of criminals holding the entire society at ransom and extorting all the good things. All the like minded people should gather little support of each other and accept the challenge of changing the world for the better. A sacrifice from each one of us will go a long way in establishing a just society. We must refurbish the society which is on the verge of becoming obsolete. We must jump into the bandwagon of those who are in the frontiers to weed out the antisocial.

We are so much embroiled in our mundane affairs, we hardly notice the deterioration that is taking place in the values of the society. It is the bounden duty of each one of us to check this malaise and take positive action in our day-to-day lives. If we lose faith in humanity then we are treading the dangerous terrain. Think hundred times, challenge your conscience and you will find that it is better to have faith rather than groping in the dark alley. Though it may sound strange, it is a fact, that we can create a paradise on earth, if we restore faith in humanity.

Anecdote

After years of cold war, Russia and America have become friends which would have been unthinkable few decades before. Two Germanys have become one.

There are signs of peace taking shape between India and Pakistan in spite of all the wars and terrorism.

At some point of time everyone has to have faith in humanity and build trust to save our planet from doomsday. Faith is the basic thing even between individuals as it is vital for any society, country and the world.

••

15

Bridge the Generation Gap

> One and one become eleven.
>
> By the time a man realizes that may be his father was right he usually has a son who thinks he is wrong – *William Wordsworth*

Generation gap is probably one of the chief causes of conflicts in the society and homes. It has always been there since time immemorial.

The ever-changing world is taking a heavy toll and playing havoc with the old generation. The speed with which lifestyle, culture, food habits, work habits, perceptions and attitudes are changing it is becoming very difficult for the older generation to cope with it.

In their lifetimes they have seen very few changes compared to the present. The difference is creating a gap between the younger and older generations. Older generation is finding it difficult to understand the new paradigm. Younger and older generations are always at loggers heads with each other. The matter is precipitating with each passing day.

There is some kind of dead end. We must educate both the generations about the old traditions and the new trends.

Japan is a classic example of both tradition and modernity. We must pick up the best from both the worlds and blend them into a beautiful synergy. We need patience, love, communication, cooperation of both the generations to bridge the gap.

The old generation should have patience and the younger generation must have respect for the older generation. We need to have some kind of institution for forging a unity between the two generations. The changes the world is unleashing is mind-boggling. We must fuse the wisdom of the old and the miracles of modernity. Contributions of both the generations is needed to achieve harmony, peace and prosperity. The dynamism of youth and the wisdom of the old can be blended to achieve extraordinary things for the benefit of the entire society.

Anecdote

Villages are still following the joint family system where everyone respects one another. The crisis today in the society is mainly because of the nuclear family. The aged are left to fend for themselves. Society is an extension of our families. Modern world is facing the crisis because of nuclear families. A person living in a joint family respects the views of others. Broken homes, juvenile crimes and divorces are the direct result of nuclear families. Elders can contribute a lot from their repository of wisdom and experience.

••

16

Take to Sports and Above All Develop Sportsman Spirit

You may win the game but lose a friend

Sports is probably one of the most important aspect of human life. The very essence of sports is to build friendship, bridge gap and bring amity between different kinds of people belonging to different parts of the world, countries and cities.

If seen in proper perspective it can melt away all animosities. Sports shapes personalities and brings emotional balance and makes you take success and defeat in the right spirit. Sports, either playing or watching makes you forget all your worries, rejuvenates and does away with the mental or physical fatigue. Sports provides fun, thrill, and excitement. Playing a team game creates in you strong bonds and friendship. Sports also brings patriotism in you when your country's team is playing with another country. Sportsmanship makes you unbiased as you appreciate the talents of players of other cities, states, countries and continents. You develop a healthy attitude towards life.

A man who is a true sportsman will face the rigors of life with a smile. His approach towards others will be healthy. Every child should be made to play outdoor sports, particularly team sports. No man is complete without sports.

Sportsmanship is more important than playing for winning. Since you may win the game and lose a friend. With so much of crass commercialization sports has been reduced to a farce losing its pristine glory.

With commercialization politics has raised its ugly head. Commercialization has lead to hooliganism and bad spirit. If sports is given its rightful place it can become a panacea for most of the enmities.

Sports must be made compulsory in all spheres of life. One of the noted persons said that let there be more and more sports in politics and less and less politics in sports. Media should also become responsible and stop encouraging partisan spirits in the masses.

Sports is an oasis in the desert of turmoil in the modern world. Sports is a colossus and stronger than anything in the world for it has the potential to make this world a better place to live and enjoy. But for sports we may have become more belligerent and cynical than we are today.

Anecdote

One of our best batsman of yesteryears G.R. Vishwanath in the golden jubilee test between India and England called back England Batsman Bob Taylor as he thought he was not out but the umpire had given him out.

Eventually for that sportive act India lost the match but that sportsman spirit is remembered till date though the match itself is forgotten. I

n one more instance Courtney Walsh of West Indies did not take the bails off when the batsman was out of the crease. West Indies lost.

In both the instances it was the sportsman spirit which won. It is the spirit which is paramount rather the result of the match.

••

17

Have Self-control

> Most powerful is he who has hmself in his own power – *Seneca*

Self-control is one of the finest attributes one should possess. Its benefits are immense. In this world full of temptations, self-control is very much essential. Without restraint we would land up in murky situations. Self-control needs to be developed gradually. Once every temptation, every provocation is resisted, you have gained self-control. Self-control once developed will immensely aid you in trying situations.

Self-control will save you in many embarrassing situations in life. Self-control is a hallmark of a truly matured and great person. Self-control will greatly aid in harmonizing relations with people. Self-control embraces the entire gamut of emotions, proclivity and negative attitude. Self-control keeps your mental, physical and spiritual health in pink. Self-control is mandatory on all frontiers viz. at work, at home, at play at public places et al.

Of late there are plethora of avenues to overspend with credit cards, easy loans etc. In today's world absence of self-control is ubiquitous. In the absence of self-control there is every chance of your landing up in the vicious circle of debts and then to financial fiasco. Make self-control your ally then see the wonders it does to your life. Developing self-control initially will look an arduous task but as you proceed further and further it will make you sure and confident of everything as you will evade all the pitfalls.

Start practicing self-control on never to react immediately to every situation. Exercise self-control in avoiding argument, gossip and back-biting. Slowly you will realize how self-control saves your precious energy. Gradually move to other spheres which you identify as your problem areas.

Anecdote

Gandhiji practiced self-control in every sphere of life. He could have vastly benefited by resorting to falsehood, but he didn't.

Telgi of stamp scam lost self-control and committed the fraud of printing fake stamp papers, insurance stamps. His greed got the better of him.

••

18

Exercise Mind, Body and Spirit

> Sound mind in a sound body

Human mind has such vast potential that it can exceed the power of whole universe provided it is kept in a good working condition. It is a precious unparalleled gift unique to human beings. Human mind can think, work at the speed of light, visualize, dream, analyze and imagine. However we need to exercise daily to keep it in excellent condition.

You can achieve anything with the help of your mind. Human mind should not be squandered on useless pursuits like fear, anger, jealousy, hatred and various other useless things. Flush out all the garbage and plant the seeds of positive thinking, creativity and dreams. Hold the reins of your mind lest it will take you to detrimental things.

Mind is a good servant and a bad master. Mind is a colossus compared even to the gigantic mountains, vast oceans and even the infinite universe. Everything pales to insignificance when compared to human mind. All the gorgeous things we see around us is the product of human mind. Human mind is vastly more superior to the fastest computers. Computers themselves are the product of human mind. Computers are extremely fast but it cannot match human mind. Thousands of years of evolution has created the human mind. Human mind can change the destiny of entire civilization. So we should give first priority to exercise the mind.

Human body is equally a beautiful and powerful engine carrying out the fiats of the human mind. However powerful the mind may be, it requires a sound body. Exercise of the body keeps diseases away. You may have a strong mind but it is of no use unless you have a strong body to enjoy life. If you do not exercise the body you will not be able to enjoy your life.

Keep away from smoking, drinking and junk food. Like mind, the present human body has gone a lot of change during the course of thousands of years of evolution. Paradoxically we take more care of our material possessions than our body. Treat your body with the respect it deserves.

Momentary temptations cause a lot of damage and it is inimical to the body. Exercise of spiritual health is also equally vital. To think positively and have positive emotions free yourself from fear worry, hatred, bias, jealousy, and anger. This keeps your spiritual health in pink. Mind, body, and spirit are the vital source for reaching the peak of human existence. Blending the three will make your life worthwhile. You can ignore one of the three at your own cost.

Human life is the rarest of rare thing nature has created. The gift is there but it solely depends on how you shape them by regular exercise. If you unleash the power of this trinity then SKY IS THE LIMIT.

Anecdote

Our cricketing legend Kapil Dev never missed an international match for want of fitness. His concentration and focus was par excellence. Take the examples of greats like Sunil Gavaskar, Sachin Tendulkar who have done India proud. It is all possible because they have made use of the trinity of mind, body and spirit.

••

19

Listen To Music

A person who hates music is capable of treason

Listening to music daily soothes the battered nerves and elevates your spirit to great heights. Listening to melodious music gives immense pleasure. Music is the food for soul as per the great littérateur William Shakespeare.

One who does not love music is capable of treason. Listening to melodious music while working enhances your efficiency. Music acts like a balm to the tired body and mind. Listening to good music makes you oblivious of the world around you.

There is no greater solace than good music to disturbed mind. It acts like a tranquilizer. Music is mellifluous to the ears. There is music everywhere around us; the chirping of birds, crowing of the cock, blowing of winds, water falls, falling rains, flowing rivers, music created by oceans. We can keep on extolling the virtues of music. Amidst all the chaos, music is the only saving grace in the world. Music epitomizes divinity.

Anecdote

According to Vedas Music can create fire, water, rain and so on. Tansen was a great exponent of such music. People were in raptures when they listened to Beatles. When you listen to the old melodious songs it makes you nostalgic.

••

20

Have Hobbies

Hobbies keep boredom away

Hobbies keep boredom away. After a grueling days work hobbies provides you the best rejuvenation and relaxation. Hobbies keep you engaged, interested, enthusiastic and leads you to ecstasy. Hobbies build common bond and healthy relationships with other people. Hobbies make your life worthwhile and purposeful. If you make hobbies your vocation then it pays you profusely in terms of money and enjoyment. Hobbies keep you mentally, emotionally and physically fit. They can bring droves of friends and admirers.

Turn your job into a hobby and you will not feel monotony, boredom and fatigue. There are plethora of hobbies you can take up. There are no dearth of hobbies. It can be philately, bird-watching, trekking, sports, reading books, listening to music, singing, playing musical instruments. The list is ad infinity. You hardly expect anything from your hobbies but they reward you in astounding proportions.

Pursuing hobbies will enrich your life beyond imagination. Have as many hobbies as possible and you will that find every moment is momentous and full of pleasure. If your job is a sedentary one then take to a hobby that involves physical efforts and if your job is physical then take to hobbies involving mental efforts.

Anecdote

Look at M.F. Hussein who converted his hobby of painting into his vocation. Daler Mehendi was an ordinary taxi-driver in U.S.A and then he transformed his hobby of singing into his profession.

••

21

Enjoy Nature

Beauty thy name is nature

Enjoying nature will fill you with joy, admiration, awe and you will be wonderstruck at the beauty of nature.

The magnificence of nature is very difficult to express in words. You will marvel, be enthralled and ecstatic when you go deeper and deeper. The more curious you become more will be unraveled. The best of man's creation cannot be compared with nature's creations. Looking at the peacock with its multi coloured body, deers, rabbits, tigers, lions, fishes and so many infinite creatures will make you astounded. The rising and setting sun with its flamboyance is simply awe-inspiring. You can watch this hours together without getting bored. Watching the tides of ocean for hours together at a stretch will not bore you. The twinkling stars and the full moon are a wonderful sight. The waterfall will fill you with so much delight that you will forget all your worries.

We must be grateful for all that nature has given to us free of cost. We are so much embroiled in mundane affairs that we do not adore the beauty of nature. The flowers, plants, trees are so soothing to the eyes that we must worship nature for all its bounty and the cornucopia.

Enjoying nature will keep you fresh throughout your iife. You will never feel tired watching and enjoying nature. Study nature in detail and you will keep marveling at its beauty. The more you enjoy nature more will you feel disgusted at the way we are eroding its magnificence.

By going against nature mankind is paying heavy price in terms of the loss of health of millions of people. Lets pledge our unstinted support to the cause of saving our beautiful nature. Plant trees and nourish them as that would be the most invaluable gift for the posterity. We must feel indebted to nature for everything we have got and contribute to its pristine glory.

Anecdote

Charles Darwin enjoyed nature so much that he kept on working at it and produced his magnum opus "Origin of Species".

Dr. Salim Ali was a great ornithologist and wrote a book on birds.

Rudyard Kipling wrote "Jungle book".

••

Be Adventurous

Braver the heart fairer the maiden

Life itself is an adventure for the daring and who pick up the gauntlet.

Adventures are so thrilling, exciting and wonderful that they add new dimensions to your life. Adventure is an elixir to life and adds purpose to your existence. Adventure props up the best in you. Adventure has the capacity to bring the best out of you and you produce extraordinary feats.

Without adventure our life would have been insipid. Climbing mountains, crossing rivers, adventure sports, roaming in the jungles are adventures which give you tremendous satisfaction and pleasure that no words are enough to describe the experience. Adventure transforms even the timid to brave-hearted.

Take time for adventure and have a tryst with yourself. Spirit of adventure in daily routine will remove boredom, fatigue and monotony from your dull daily routine. Adventure will elevate you to great heights winning you accolades, rewards and fame.

Adventure removes all the inhibitions you normally nurture. Adventure requires the harmony between body, mind and spirit. Practice spirit of adventure in every facet of your life to enjoy every moment of life. Leave no room for fear, worry and melancholy.

Anecdote

Edmund Hilary and Sherpa Tenzing Norgay were the first to conquer the highest peak of the world, the Mount Everest. Many people crossed the English Channel. Columbus was a great adventurer who discovered America.

••

23

Have Enthusiasm for Good Things

> Enthusiasm burns all obstacles

Enthusiasm, it is said burns all obstacles. One can succeed at anything for which one has unlimited enthusiasm. Enthusiasm for positive things and good things rewards you amply. Enthusiasm is a very potent weapon even if you lack the skills. Some people have abundant enthusiasm when it comes to criticizing, condemning, complaining, gossiping and backbiting. Enthusiasm blended with positive attitude is excellent but if it is blended with negative attitude it is devastating.

Enthusiasm can be best described as under :

Enthusiasm brings Energy

Energy brings Efficiency

Efficiency brings Effectiveness

Effectiveness brings Euphoria

Boundless enthusiasm transforms into a dynamite that you can achieve anything you set your hands on. When a person is possessed with enthusiasm he is capable of incredible things. Enthusiasm sets in motion tremendous energy that you will never get fatigued by any amount of work. Absence of enthusiasm makes you lazy, indolent, intolerant and tired. Boredom is nothing but lack of enthusiasm. Enthusiasm makes a person energetic and focused and nothing is beyond the realms of possibility.

Anecdote

Dev Anand actor of yester years is known for his enthusiasm to make films on various themes. Today when he is no more, we still cherish his enthusiasm.

Even his growing age had not lessened his enthusiasm. People with enthusiasm keep on doing things they love the most.

••

24

Always Look for Solutions and Never be Part of the Problem

> A person looking for solution always treats a knock as an opportunity and the person part of problem treats it as noise

Problem itself contains its solution. Solution germinates from a problem. There is no problem that cannot be solved. Though it is at times intractable but it can be mitigated even if not fully solved.

Problems must be taken by their horns. Write down the problem, analyze, discuss with your well-wishers and half the problem will be solved.

Worrying about a problem exacerbates the problem. Never panic, as it clouds your judgment and your ability to think clearly. Looking for solution takes the sting out of the problem. Break the problem into pieces and find solutions bit by bit. Problems, it is said are opportunities in works clothes. Problem is like a pebble; when it is brought near the eyes it clouds your vision but taken away from eyes it looks small.

Remain unruffled, cool, composed and write down the possible solutions. Even if it is not solved take the counsel of experts or those who have undergone the same problem. No man is without problems. But it is the reaction to the problem that makes you meek or formidable.

Problems are nature's way to test your courage and fortitude. Problems, no doubt, cannot be wished away but some solution can certainly be found. Never press the panic buttons when confronted with a problem. Face it squarely and test all your faculties to solve the problem.

Anecdote

> ***Dr. Helen Keller was blind from birth but she was not overawed by the problem. Instead she wrote many books for the blind. Edison was deaf but look at the number of inventions he made. It is your perception and not the problem that is responsible for a problem.***

••

Take Quick Decisions and Act Promptly

> Taking quick decisions is a sign of courage and
> to act promptly; supreme confidence

Taking quick decisions is vital for success in any endeavour. Certain moments are so critical calling for split second decision that they do not offer any time. Indecisiveness is a sign of weakness and decisiveness is a sign of temerity.

No body can vouch on the consequence of any decision – whether our decision was right or wrong. Quick decision removes all fear, doubt, worry, confusion in your mind. Any decision requires immediate action or else the decision dies a premature death.

Some people are inveterate indecisive persons that they can never decide under the pretext that they are analyzing the pros and cons. Take decisions quickly and change it slowly as advised by the great business magnate Henry Ford. Every decision changes your life either for better or worse. But do not be overawed by that as you cannot keep procrastinating taking decisions.

Make it a habit to taking quick decisions as that is the key to success. Decisions shape your destiny. Acquire knowledge from various sources on varied subjects as that would lay the foundation to taking decisions fast and accurately. Emulate successful people. Take decisions quickly, act upon them but don't blame anybody for your decisions. Take responsibility for your decisions and actions. Taking quick decisions, acting upon them and achieving success will make you formidable.

Anecdote

Henry Ford took the decision to make eight-cylinder engine and asked his engineers to keep on trying. He took the decision and did not change even in the face of failure. Ultimately after a year of efforts and millions of dollars spent on the project, it yielded the result. He could design the eight-cylinder engine.

••

26

Have Dignity of Labour

> Mocking at lowly jobs is a sign of immaturity

Work is the single most factor which has transformed monkey into mankind. No work, however menial, is bad but it is the approach that makes the difference. Only when man started using his hand that he developed the brain.

So never mock or contempt any work however much petty it looks. Have dignity of labour. Respect all persons however lowly work he may be doing because all the work in a society is important. Imagine if no sweeper were there, how ugly and filthy every place would have looked like.

Persons born to illiterate and poor families have no choice but to take on menial jobs for keeping the body and soul together. All kinds of people are required to run the society. If you enjoy your job in spite of it being a lowly one you will do it with enthusiasm. Always find new ways to do the job. You will earn the respect of others and you will be richly rewarded.

Smile at your work and it will smile back at you. You frown at your work and you will find the work boring and monotonous.

Don't despise any work but look at it as a necessity of life and you will understand the deep meaning of work. Work done with dignity and devotion will elevate your spirit and morale and you will derive immense pleasure.

Treat work as an opportunity to serve the society and you will enjoy your work to the most. Work is a magic wand which can bring you material, physical and spiritual riches. Only work can give you food, clothing, shelter and self-satisfaction. As it is said there are no free lunches in the society. Work is as mellifluous as honey. Once you get addicted to work, you will find so much pleasure you cannot describe in words.

Anecdote

Late Dhirubhai Ambani was a mere petrol pump attendant and did not scoff at the work but dreamt of becoming the owner of oil company. Ultimately he became one. Gandhiji did his own toilet cleaning but he became great because he had dignity of labour.

••

Aspire to Succeed but Do Not Compromise

> A success without ethics is worse than a failure

To aim for success is not a crime but to compromise on principles and ethics, certainly is. Always have qualms of conscience and never forsake of morality.

Many people have an obsession with success that they compromise on principles and ethics. They will stoop to any level to achieve success. It is better to fail than to compromise on principles.

If you achieve success by compromising on principles you will lose the respect of society. Compromising on principles for the sake of success will not give you the kind of satisfaction you were aspiring for. There is always the chance of landing in trouble. Of late, trend is to grow rich overnight by means fair or foul. Seeking success at any cost is dangerous to the individual as well as to the society.

Different people have different definitions of success. You must define your own success and should not blindly ape other people. Success need not be in material terms but it can be non-material also. If you resort to shortcuts involving compromises, your conscience will torment you day in and day out.

Share your success with others and never get intoxicated by your success as that may prove to be your nemesis. In fact your agenda for success should be in harmony with the benefit of the society. Such a success will earn you friends, material riches and accolades. You are assured of success if your aspirations will help the society at large. Emulate the examples of great people.

Anecdote

Take the example of Bill Gates, Narayanmurthy, Amitabh Bacchan whose success has made the people better off due to their contribution to the society. No body will mind Bill Gates being the richest man in the world as Microsoft has made millions of people's work easy. Every time you use Word, Excel you are astounded by their utility.

••

28

Self-introspection – An Invaluable Tool

A person who probes within finds the god within

Self-introspection is so valuable that one cannot overemphasize the fact. Spend sometime daily to exercise self-introspection as it will greatly enrich you mentally and spiritually. It provides you with the unique opportunity to analyze your strengths and weaknesses.

Utilize your free time to do self-introspection and gain immensely. When travelling alone introspect to get an insight into your personality. By resorting to introspection you need not depend upon any outer source to know yourself.

You are your best friend provided you make use of self-introspection. It removes all garbage from your mind and increases your thinking ability. It greatly aids in fathoming the depths of your personality. Introspection helps getting rid of your worries, fears, confusion and makes you think lucidly. With this valuable tool you can chisel yourself to greatness.

You will never have boring moments in life if you have the habit of self-introspection.

Anecdote

Gandhiji made great use of this tool or else he would not have been able to become great and written his autobiography "My Experiments With Truth". Socrates became a great philosopher because of self-introspection.

••

Do Not Have Complexes

To show superiority is disguised inferiority complex

Do not have any type of complex. It is advised not to have either inferiority complex or superiority complex. If you have inferiority complex then you will not feel confident before others. You will not feel comfortable with your self. You will always suffer silently and feel withdrawn. This will affect your working and your morale will always be very low. People will also berate you and humiliate you every now and then. It will be very ominous to your self-respect. You will always be disconcerted when communicating with others. You will never have the courage to stand up and speak with others.

On the other hand superiority complex will create problems with others. They will brand you as haughty. Others will try to avoid you as your complex will make them feel uncomfortable. Superiority about yourself will make you an egoist.

Your nature will be one of condescence. Your behaviour will be overpowering. It is said that even superiority complex is a form of inferiority complex. To be bereft of complex will make you respect others and yourself. You will have healthy relationships with all the people and will immensely enhance your personality and success. Having a complex is a sign of weakness and abnormality. Be balanced and you will have unbridled success and host of friends.

Anecdote

The Germans had superiority complex of being the superior race. They had alienated people of other countries. Hitler decimated thousands of Jews during second world war. Even in India higher caste people had superiority complex but that has become counterproductive and proved to be disadvantageous for the entire society.

••

30

Have Sense of Humour

Humour can cure any malady

Having sense of humour is the greatest tranquilizer in the world. It saves a lot of heartburn. It is a silver lining in a dark cloud. Humour is very unique to human beings. Sense of humour is very much a saving grace in times of grim situations. It removes the monotony of any situation. Humour reduces the tension. You will always be cheerful if you have a strong sense of humour.

Humour is one of the rare quality that adds a new dimension to your personality. You will be the most sought after person in parties and get-togethers. Humour these days is a very vital element of human life as there is lot of stress everywhere.

Anecdote

Tenali Raman and Birbal are quite well-known to the people of India for their sense of humour and wit. Once Tenali wanted to expose a King's servant who was very corrupt. Tenali once was going to the King's Court to manifest his

skill. He met the corrupt servant at the gate and promised him half of what he would get as gift from the king.

Tenali Raman displayed his skill. The king was very much impressed by Tenali and asked him to choose any reward. Tenali Raman requested him to give him 100 lashes. The king was intrigued but on the insistence of Tenali he ordered the flogging. As soon as 50 lashes were given Tenali requested the king to stop. Tenali went outside and brought the corrupt servant inside the court and requested to give lashes to the corrupt servant. Everyone was bamboozled. Tenali explained that he had promised half the share of his reward. Everyone in the court were in splits and admired Tenali's sense of humour.

••

Be Slow to Promise and Quick to Fulfill

Pran Jaye Par Vachan Na Jaye (Let life go but do not break a promise)

Always keep your promise and never go back on your promise as that would irreparably damage your reputation. In Hindi there is a popular saying *Jaan jaye par vachan na jaye* meaning let even life go but do not let the promise be broken. It is better not to promise anything than promising and doing nothing. Promise and performance is an arduous task which very few people can deliver. Politicians keep on promising at the time of elections and never bother to keep them. Trusting politicians is like trusting a fox. Promising raises hope and expectation but breaking them breaks many hearts. If you keep promising and fail to keep them, it will make people never to take you seriously.

Anecdote

Our late beloved Prime Minsiter Lal Bahadur Shastri was known to keep his promises. He went to Tashkent Russia to have peace talks with the Prime Minsiter of Pakistan and he never returned. His death is shrouded in mystery till date but he kept his promise. ••

32

Be Free from Vices

> Virtue is its own reward and vices are gateway to hell

If you are free from vices naturally you will develop healthy habits.

Once you become a chain smoker, alcoholic, gambler or any other addict your life's energy is dissipated and you lose all the good things in life – wealth, relation and energy. You are left with no verve to enjoy good things in life in addition to spoiling your health and wealth.

Human life is too precious to be wasted on vices. Just because you have not tasted the better things that you fall into the vicious circle of vices. Human life is worth too much to be squandered on vices. Having a worthwhile purpose in life is very much essential to feel worthy of human life. Vices puts you in a quagmire from which it is very difficult to come out.

Think thousand times before you fall prey to vices. Human life is the greatest gift and it is atrocious to subject it to vices. For want of clear purpose in life, vices fill the vacuum. Indulgence in vices gives momentary pleasure but in the long run they cause havoc with the lives of people. Many a kings have lost their kingdoms because of one solitary vice. The very word vice suggests that it has a vice-like grip on the person harboring it. Advice is to avoid the vice. You will be healthy, wealthy and wise if you are free from vice.

Anecdote

As per Hindu mythology Pandavas lost their kingdom along with the honour of Draupati as they indulged in gambling. Even the mightiest are not free from foibles. The mighty Ravana was killed by Lord Rama because of his obsession with Sita.

••

Be Disciplined

A disciplined person is bereft of problems

Following a disciplined life is a very tough job but it keeps you healthy, wealthy and wise. The Universe follows a very disciplined path. The earth has been orbiting the Sun for millions of years in the same pattern. Sun rise, sun set and nature follows a disciplined rhythm.

Human beings also should follow discipline in their daily routine otherwise the implications are fraught with danger. If you break the discipline in any sphere you have to pay a heavy price. Physical, mental, spiritual and financial discipline is very much necessary to achieve success in life.

It may be very difficult to follow discipline but in the long run it rewards you richly. Self-discipline is better than external discipline. Everyone scoffs at external discipline. Even children rebel against external discipline.

Anecdote

According to the Hindu Epic Mahabharata, Arjun became an ace archer because he was highly disciplined. When the coach Dronacharya asked his disciples to aim at the target none of them was accurate in describing the target except Arjuna.

In the modern days Kapil Dev our champion cricketer was so highly disciplined that he never missed a match on the grounds of fitness.

••

34

Karmanye Vadikaraste
Ma Phaleshu Kada chana

> Boya beej babul ka tho aam kahanse hoi
> (You cannot reap mangoes if you had sown cactus)

These are the famous lines of Lord Krishana in his discourse Srimad Bhagwad Gita. This is an oft quoted but most misunderstood quote. It is not to mean that you keep on working and not expect anything. It means that at the time of doing something do not expect any reward as that would disturb your focus and you will mess up the work. You neither finish the work properly nor get the reward. You need to have full focus and concentration at the time of doing anything.

Be focused while doing the work and the rewards will automatically ensue. This quote has a scientific and logical base. If you get the essence you will benefit a lot. No body will ask you to keep on doing your work and not expect anything in return as that would take away the motivation.

Anecdote

Suppose a batsman in a cricket match is performing before a packed stadium and intends to win the accolades without concentration and wants to hit a six he is very likely to get out. This is because his focus is on the rewards rather than the performance. First perform and then think of rest.

••

35

Strive For Excellence

> Continuous striving for excellence is the key to success and satisfaction

Always keep striving for excellence in whatever you do. You will find everything interesting and there will be no boring moments in your life in addition to rewards. Japanese kaizan technique is an art of making constant improvements in whatever you do. Striving for excellence will keep you busy in finding innovative methods to do the same thing.

Most of the people find their jobs boring because they do not try to make constant improvements. Always aiming at excellence will keep you lively and energetic and you will almost become indispensable. In every sphere you try to excel. There is a wrong notion that one can excel in only one field. Keep on improving your job skill, communication skill, and social skill you will certainly excel in any field you choose. Whether you achieve success or not but the very pursuit of excelling will give you immense pleasure and recognition. Reading of *The Sky is the limit* by Dr. Wayne Dyer is recommended.

Anecdote

Cricketers of yester years Navjyotsingh Siddhu, Sunil Gavaskar, Shastri, Geoff Boycott, Tony Greig, Richie Benaud and the like excelled in playing and are now ace commentators.

Ronald Reagan made a mark in both films and was the President of United States of America. Another example is that of Mr. Universe Arnold Schwarzenegger after making his name in body-building became a successful actor and now has become the Governor of California.

There are many examples. You need to focus on whatever you are doing in the present.

••

36

Have KID In Your Personality

> Having KID in you is worth the world

First what is KID? K stands for Knowledge, I stands for integrity and D stands for Devotion.

You need to have all the three in abundant quantity. If you have knowledge and integrity and do not have devotion then you will not succeed. Imagine you are knowledgeable and have integrity but do not devote your time to finish off your work. What will be the result? It is obvious you will not succeed. Nobody is going to reward you because you are knowledgeable and integrity is unquestionable as you have not produced the desired result. Now, suppose you have the knowledge and devotion but do not have integrity then you will produce result but your reputation is tarnished since nobody trusts you. Have you achieved success? Obviously no. Suppose you have absolute integrity and devotion and lack knowledge then also you will not be able to deliver the goods.

It is crystal clear that you need to have KID in you to succeed in any endeavour.

Anecdote

Again let us take the example of Harshad Mehta. He had knowledge and devotion but the most vital ingredient, Integrity, was conspicuously missing.

There are umpteen number of examples of this. Many people fail for want of knowledge and devotion as people in general have integrity in ample measure.

••

37

Develop Language, Logic And Dynamism

> Man is a bundle of dynamite more powerful than the most powerful nuclear bomb

Language, logic and dynamism are the gunpowder mixture to break the hardest rock. Language gives you the understanding of any subject. The more fluent you are the more articulate you are and your power of communication is tremendous. Logic gives you the analytical power to analyse any situation instead of getting trapped in emotional quagmire. Dynamism adds fire to both language and logic. If any element is missing you can not succeed in any negotiation.

Imagine you have language and logic but lack the dynamism you will keep the ideas to yourself as you will lack the audacity to express your views. If you have language and dynamism but lack logic you can never put up your views cogently. If you have logic and dynamism and not language then you will not put the things properly in a manner understood by others.

Anecdote

You take any Amitabh movie – you will find the right blend of the vital trinity of language, logic and dynamism. Boldness has power, genius and magic. All the successful people have these qualities in copious measure. Logic can remove the mist of mystery shrouded on any intractable problem and solve it. But for logic human beings could not have made so much of progress.

Needless to mention the importance of language as it is the medium through which all ideas are expressed. The portentous contribution made to the knowledge, wisdom gathered is because of language only. But for language no progress can be made.

••

Keep Smiling And Keep Winning

A smiling face wins lot of friends

Smile, it is said, improves your face value. Put on your face a smile and walk thousands of mile. Smile improves your personality. Smile wins many friends in day-to-day life. If you smile at a rank stranger he also returns a smile. If you wear a frown you can never wear a crown. However annoyed the other person may be your smile assuages his hurt. Smiling is good for your health as well. An enchanting smile makes the other person put back the drawn sword into his sheath. Smile removes the wrinkles from your face. Frowning requires 70 muscles but a smile on the contrary removes stress.

Smile is a unique attribute to human beings. Make the most of it for your own benefit. A salesman with a smile wins many an order. A smiling face, like a magnet, attracts people. Keep smiling and keep winning.

Anecdote

Leonardo Da Vinci's magnum opus Mona Lisa adores many a homes for its smile.

If you look at a mirror while you are frowning you look like a demon whereas a smile makes you look like an angel. A look at an innocent smile of a child will make you forget all your worries.

••

39

Success is a Journey, Not a Destination

Success is an ongoing and never ending process

Success is a journey you undertake and it certainly is not a destination. After you reach the acme, more than the success you relish the journey. You become nostalgic about the initial hesitation and the slow trickle of odyssey. Once you succeed you tend to become complacent. You must not rest on your past laurels but set new goals for achievement. Keep on making pleasant struggle in your life. You will enjoy the journey more than the success. Once you achieve success you forget all the travails and anguish you suffered. Even if you fail you have walked some distance towards your goal. Nature has built into every human being the ability to attain one's goal and success. Don't keep making excuses like your lack of education, money, opportunity etc. There are innumerable examples in the world of those who have succeeded in spite of all the handicaps. Success is a perpetual journey with infinite destinations.

You must have experienced during journey by train, bus, plane how beautiful is the journey itself. You meet lot of people, halt at many stations before your final destination comes. Same is the case with the journey of life and success. ••

Self-discipline is the Best Discipline

> A self-disciplined person needs no rod

If you are a self-respecting person you will love to have self-discipline instead of discipline being imposed by others. When discipline is imposed from outside it damages your self-respect and image. In any sphere self-discipline is essential to avoid unpleasantness. If office timings are say 10 o'clock, you be there ten minutes before rather than ten minutes late. If you have to catch a train, bus, plane if you reach late you will end up missing the train, bus or plane. Be it an appointment with a doctor, important person, friend, be there at the place before the appointed time. All these comes with self-discipline. Universe also follows self-discipline otherwise there would be destruction and devastation. Self-discipline is both essential and enjoyable as it is a prerequisite for success in any endeavour.

Anecdote

You take the example of successful people from any field they always had self-discipline. Likes of Sunil Gavaskar, Sachin Tendulkar, Amitabh Bacchan, Gandhiji, all were and some of them are even now highly self-disciplined.

41

Be *Man Se Bhakt* And *Acharan Se Sant*

A hand that serves is better than the lips which preach divinity

Sant Kabir said that one should be devoted from the heart and by behaviour a saint. There is no point in worshipping for hours together and then cheating people in day-to-day life. The very essence of worship is to make you more humane.

You may read scriptures, worship and be a mercenary; then all your godliness is futile. One should practice what one preaches. Example is better than precept. Religion is meant to make a person more modest and humane. You should not confine your goodness only when in the precincts of sacred place but carry it to all the places. A truly religious person will have respect for people of other religions. All bloodshed in the name of religion is hypocrisy and vitiates the very essence and purpose of religion.

Anecdote

In the midst of voluminous tax evasion Sachin Tendulkar was awarded a certificate for being an honest tax-payer. This should be an eye-opener for others to emulate his example. Gandhiji lead a Spartan living to set an example for others to emulate. Naturally he had so much of following. We may not agree with some of his teachings but he cannot be accused of opportunism and what goes on in the name of social work.

••

42

An Ounce of Help is Better Than a Ton of Advice

A timely help is better than wordy advice

You must have seen many people who are ready with advice in times of emergency, crisis and difficult situation but when it comes to doing concrete things even a miniscule contribution is not forthcoming from them. Giving advices is the favourite pastime of many but actually giving helping hand is a rarity. You be one of those who do their mite for the needy and desolate.

Anecdote

As per the Hindu Great Epic Ramayana when Lord Ram had to cross the ocean to Sri Lanka, a small squirrel soiled itself and immersed the soil in ocean to construct the dam. Lord Ram was greatly impressed by the attitude of the little squirrel and caressed the squirrel with his three fingers and it is believed that from that day the squirrels have three stripes on their bodies.

• •

43

Always Have Same Standards For Yourself And Others

Practise what you preach

It is a common practice, without our knowing, that we have one set of rules for others and one set of rules for ourselves. Same mistake which we do not brook in others we commit them blatantly.

Many a times we criticize others but when we are criticized we take offence. We tell others should always tell the truth but we find it convenient to tell lies when it suits us. Each person tells only that thing which is convenient to him. Politicians tell people to exercise austerity but there is no end to their profligacy.

It takes rare courage to admit this fault in ourselves. But if you remove this anomaly you will have removed one of your erroneous zones. You will be at peace with yourself if you acquire this quality. You will never find yourself in any awkward situation.

You will have many admirers and will be the cynosure of all eyes.

Anecdote

Gandhiji, Nelson Mandela, Dr. Martin Luther King practiced what they preached. They were statesman and saint par excellence. They could have rolled in wealth had they followed double standards but they preferred not to do so.

••

44

Use Time To Enrich Yourself In All Respects

> Kal ghela pudhe baghit me rahilo (I kept looking and the time went by.)

Time and tide wait for none.

Time probably is more precious than any other thing in the world. Everyone in the world has the same twenty-four hours to himself. Time is limited and very valuable to be spent on useless things. A busy person finds time for everything. Time once gone can never be reclaimed. Even money is less valuable than time, since money can be earned back but not time. No body, however mighty, can retrieve the time once gone. Make judicious use of time in enriching yourself by reading books, making friends, and self-improvement . Time wasted on futile talk is an atrocious waste of time.

Time spent on gossiping, criticizing, back-biting can be better utilized to enrich yourself. Use time for work, pleasure, hobbies, listening to music and meeting people. Using time for self-improvement will pay rich dividends. Time judiciously used will save you from crisis. Start early and reach in time in all spheres of life. Time management is one of the most useful skill to master. Proper time management will save you from difficult situations. Use atleast one hour for reading good books and one hour for planning the day's work. Wasting time is as good as wasting life. Manage your time and life will manage itself. It is advised by author Pereira that we should allocate 8 hours for work, 8 hours for sleep and 8 hours for leisure. Too much or too little will upset the harmony. You may allocate as per your convenience and comfort.

Anecdote

Benjamin Franklin is the best example who used his precious time to build his personality. . His thirteen tenets to improve your personality will be very useful :

1) ***Temperance – Eat not to dullness; Drink not to elevation.***
2) ***Silence – Speak not but what may benefit others or yourself; avoid trifling conversation.***
3) ***Order – Let all your things have their places; let each part of your business have its time.***
4) ***Resolution – Resolve to perform what you ought, perform without fail what you resolve.***
5) ***Frugality – Make no expense but to do good to others or yourself, i.e. waste nothing.***
6) ***Industry – Lose no time; be always employed in something useful; cut off all unnecessary actions.***
7) ***Sincerely – Use no hurtful deceit; think innocently and justly, and if you speak, speak accordingly.***

8) *Justice – Wrong none by doing injuries, or omitting the benefits that are your duty.*

9) *Moderation – Avoid extremes; forbear resenting injuries so much as you think they deserve.*

10) *Cleanliness – Tolerate no uncleanliness in body, clothes, or habitation.*

11) *Tranquility – Be not disturbed at trifles, or at accidents common or unavoidable.*

12) *Chastity – Rarely use venery but for health or offspring; never to dullness, weakness or the injury of your own or another's peace or reputation.*

13) *Humility – Imitate Jesus and Socrates.*

Blend Materialism with Spiritualism

A man cannot live by bread alone
In recent times there is a mad rush to accumulate riches

In the blind pursuit of materialism the casualties are ethics and human relations and consideration. You may amass wealth but lose peace and human relations. You may even rub the law on the wrong side. Materialism out of bounds will force you to take to wrong practices. You will buy things for which you have no use or have two pieces of the same like two cars, two flats, two televisions etc.

Once you are possessed with materialism you tend to forget the limits. So it is necessary to blend it with spiritualism. Spiritualism aids you in keeping proper balance, happiness, peace, human relations, good moral conduct and be free from vices. Spiritualism may also mean helping other people in times of their difficulties and also doing good for the needy and desolate.

However, too much of spiritualism may also land you in trouble in the sense you lose interest in the day-to-day affairs and treat materialism with scant respect. Proper blend of spiritualism and materialism is a must to live life worthwhile. Moderation in everything is necessary to maintain harmony.

Anecdote

A famous story of a person in "How Much Land Does a Man Need" by Leo Tolstoy needs to be quoted here.

A man went to buy a farm land from a businessman. The deal was fixed. The buyer could acquire as much land as he could by running from sunrise to sunset on the vast land. He became very much greedy and started running very far in the hope that he will acquire a vast tract of land. He kept on exerting himself and finally covered a long round but when he reached back to the point from where he started he was totally exhausted and fell dead at the starting point.

Moral of the story is that avarice is detrimental to your well-being. You must exert only to the extent you can manage.

••

46

Don't Fall Victim to Superstition

Sweekara tumhi Gyan aani Vigyan

Door kara Andhshraddha aani Agyan

(Accept knowledge and science and keep away illiteracy and superstition)

Superstition is very common to human-beings inspite of tremendous advancement in science. Superstitions were born centuries ago when human-beings did not have enough logic to explain the phenomenon and hence attributed everything to superstitions. People related a happening to some other thing which had no relation.

In the past two things must have happened together hence they were correlated. So when something happens it is assumed it will follow the same pattern as in the past. Like a cat crossing your path and your work not getting done. It must have so happened in the past that a cat must have crossed someone's path and his work did not get done. It must have happened two or three times and it became an established fact. The same is the case with number thirteen. It is considered to be unlucky. But it is not so.

Every happening in the world has cause and effect logic. Even though if we assume superstitions to be true it is better not to believe as not believing in them will improve confidence in yourself without depending upon any outside source. Give a try to once believe in rational thinking and the amount of good it does to your confidence. Don't wait for auspicious occasion to start something good since opportunities rarely come again. There is a Sanskrit saying "Shubast Shikram" meaning whatever is good must be started immediately. One more saying is "opportunities seized multiply and when neglected they die".

Anecdote

Once a farmer kept on waiting for the auspicious occasion to sow the seed. He kept on waiting and the monsoon came and went. Other farmers sowed the seed and harvested in bounty but this farmer kept on waiting and did not get anything.

••

47

Rolling Stone Gathers a Lot of Moss

A migrating person grows healthy wealthy and wise

The age-old saying is *Rolling Stone Gathers No Moss*. However times have changed. These days migration from one place to another makes you stronger in all fields. You become more adaptable, flexible and formidable. Each time you go to a new place, you develop all your mental faculties to deal with changing culture, tradition, style, language and climatic conditions. You get to know new people, new culture, different natural places, variety of cuisines and so many other things.

In your own place you tend to be very complacent as in times of emergency you have your friends, relatives, family members to rely on. Whereas in a new place you have to start afresh and you bring out the best in yourself. Stagnant water becomes moribund and stinks whereas flowing water is always fresh and full of minerals. In the same way a person who keeps changing places develops lot of skills and becomes a complete man. He also in the process sheds prejudices about other people, their ethos and habits. You mingle with varied people and broaden your horizon.

Anecdote

In our own country people from Kerala are very migratory type and adapt themselves to new places like fish to water. They travel far and wide and are very successful. So many Keralites are settled in the Gulf and are remitting valuable foreign currency to India. Jews settled in U.S.A. are doing wonderfully well. It is always found that people settling away from their native places are faring better than the locals. It is because they are oblivious of the opportunities locally available.

••

48

Fate-way is The Way to Your Doom

Tuch Aahe Tujya Jivanacha Shilpakar
(You are the architect of your own fate)

It is said that Man is the Architect of His Own Fate. It is amply clear that if a man decides he can carve a niche for himself and is doomed if he believes in things like fate. A weak man will always consult astrologers, palmists, numerologists to know his fate. I do not want to get into any controversy over whether these studies are scientific or irrational. But rarely the predictions come true. There are many charlatans in these fields exploiting the gullible masses. At least to my knowledge I am yet to come across a futurologist giving a precise prediction.

There are umpteen number of examples of people ruining their lives seeking the advices of astrologers. It is better to believe in your strength than your stars as that would give you more satisfaction in achieving your cherished dreams with planning and efforts.

Every human being has a Magic Wand in himself to turn everything into gold and that magic wand is your own burning desire – the will to believe in your dream and take positive action in that direction.

Anecdote

There are so many marital relations gone sour even after comparing meticulously their horoscopes and also there are many marriages thriving inspite of not matching the horoscopes.

Our own Late Dhirubhai Ambani rose from rags to riches. He was an attendant at a petrol pump when he dreamt of becoming the owner of an oil company and ultimately reached his goal. Bill Gates the richest man in the world instead of pursuing his studies went in pursuit of his dream of creating a wonderful software and the rest is history. Kroc of the MacDonald fame hardly had a $20 in his pocket when he dreamt of MacDonald chain of hotels.

That is the power of dream. They never consulted any astrologer or believed in their fate but firmly believed in their dreams and dared to act on them. Burning Desire, the will, goal, enthusiasm, unstinted pursuit and positive action can conquer fate.

••

49

Khudi ko kar buland itna
ke har taqder se pehle
khuda bande se khud puche
ki bata teri raza kya hai

You must awake the giant within you to reach your goal

There is no greater Alladin's Lamp than this mantra. This mantra means that you make yourself so strong that Almighty Himself will ask what you wish at the beginning of every endeavour. These are the famous lines of Poet Iqbal in admiration of the inimitable Chatrapati Shivaji Maharaj.

Every human being has the ability to build himself into a colossus that he can achieve anything in the world provided he has the will. Don't make any excuse. You can either make an excuse or be successful. The choice is entirely yours. Fortunately there are many books to guide you to your goal. To name a few *Think and Grow Rich* by Napolean Hill, *The Power of Positive Thinking* by Dr. Norman Vincent Peal, *The Magic of Thinking Big* by David Schwartz, *You, Inc.* by Burke Hedges, *How to Win Friends and Influence People* by Dale Carnegie, *You Can Win* by Shiv Khera and lot many.

All these books need to be read, understood, digested and implemented to achieve your dreams.

Anecdote

Abraham Lincoln the famous President of America achieved success after failing so many times. Edison, Henry Ford, Alexander The Great, Chatrapati Shivaji all were giants achieving whatever they visualized. Of late Sachin Tendulkar, Rahul Dravid, Yuvraj Singh, Usain Bolt, Steve Waugh, Michael Jordan, Pete Sampras, David Beckham,Vishwanathan Anand, Michael Schumacher, Roger Federer, Lance Armstrong have achieved whatever they set their sights on. Bill Gates has risen and still rising whatever he wishes to dizzy heights. Last but not the least Mathematical Genius Ramanujam did wonders in Maths inspite of having no formal qualifications.

Every man is endowed with the same power to reach great heights if only he takes himself seriously and not to deride himself. It is said that no one can make you feel inferior without your permission.

••

Your Success is Directly Proportional to Your Failure Rate

The more you fail the more you are destined to succeed

Most of the people when they fail once give up their efforts to reach their goal without realizing that a failure is the stepping stone for success. The more you fail the more you should learn and make a comeback. You may lose the battles but you should concentrate on winning the war. Ultimately it is not the strong or weak but the person who thinks that he will win wins. Keep on failing and of course if you learn and move forward, success is assured. Success is not solely meant to mean material success but success in any of your chosen fields.

Anecdote

Once upon a time a king who was defeated six times hided himself in a cave. There he saw a spider trying to spin a web but was not successful. However on its seventh attempt it was successful. The king took the inspiration from the spider, mustered courage and gathered his army once again and defeated his arch enemy.

••

51

There is More to Life than Money

If money were everything than every person would be happy; rich men have their own problems

There is a common belief that all problems can be solved with money. Money, no doubt, is very important but it is not the end. It also depends upon how judiciously you use the money. Money may make you haughty and supercilious. It may also spoil good relations. Money causes many heartburns and builds chasm between human relations. Money is a good servant and a bad master. If you are profligate you will end up being a pauper. Money spent on vices will prove to be your nemesis. Money wisely spent can bring you lot of satisfaction.

Money

Money can buy you sycophants but not friends

Money can buy you luxuries but not comforts

Money can buy you everything but not parents

Money can buy you cozy beds but not sleep

Money can buy you books but not knowledge

There is no greater pleasure than thinking said Edison. You can never measure the kind of pleasure you derive by reading a good book or doing a selfless help which any amount of money cannot buy. True happiness, smile, and the innocence of children can never be bought with money.

There are so many things in the world that any amount of money cannot buy. No need to lament if you have everything but money. If you have everything you can earn money but money cannot buy everything.

Anecdote

Gandhiji was called a half-naked fakir but he had everything a man may desire. The great Tamil sage poet Thiruvalluvar wrote the inimitable Thirukural encompassing every facet of life. It contains so much of wisdom. Sant Gnyaneshwar wrote Gnyaneshwari, Valmiki wrote the great Indian epic Ramayana. Sant Kabir wrote so many dohas, William Shakespeare wrote so many classics. These people derived so much of pleasure writing these classics that money was secondary to them.

••

52

$$\text{Happiness} = \frac{\text{Efforts}}{\text{Expectations}}$$

Happiness is a state of mind

When you have least expectations from your efforts you suffer less frustration. High expectations from any endeavour leads to frustration if the results or rewards are not proportionate to your expectations. If you expect the least and get more in return your happiness is boundless. It is always advised to expect the least as that will assure you happiness. This formula needs to be firmly entrenched in your mind as that would give you timely help.

Anecdote

In the Cricket World Cup of 1983 India scored a meager 183 which was within easy reach of the mighty West Indies but eventually Indians won the world cup. The people of India were in raptures and ecstasy as they had least expected.

••

53

Discontentment is the Road to Progress

> Discontentment is the mother of progress
>
> The popular belief is that contentment leads to happiness
>
> Contentment comes more because of "Grapes Are Sour" thinking

Had man been content with what he had we would never have seen so much development and progress we witness today. Discontentment to some extent is necessary to make you probe deeper into things. Contentment for material possessions is alright but contentment in acquiring knowledge should never be there.

Contentment mostly creeps in when one resigns to one's fate. Contentment makes you lazy and you never strive hard to attain your cherished goals.

Discontentment makes you put stress on all your faculties which otherwise would have remained dormant. If you want to make your life worthwhile then you certainly need to be discontented. Discontentment makes you curious and fantasize. All the inventions and discoveries in the world have germinated from one virtue that is discontentment. Discontentment for the right reason is advised.

Anecdote

Edison carried out 10000 experiments before he invented the electric bulb. Had he remained contented then we would have been, probably deprived of lights. A

ll scientific research is born out of discontentment.

••

54

Vanquish the Hidden Enemy Within You

> Anger does more harm to the one harbouring it than the one who is the target. To be angry in the right measure at the right time for the right reason at the right person is the greatest challenge – *Aristotle*

You need to keep your temper in check lest it goes beyond control and makes you a beast. An angry man cannot be trusted with a weapon. Anger in moderation is like a lamp which provides illumination in darkness where anger in excess is like a conflagration which burns the source and the surrounding. So many wrongs are done at the heat of the moment for which we repent later. Jealousy is a green monster within you which nibbles at your energy. Ego is another vice which retards progress. Ego gives many some temporary delight but it is detrimental to your progress.

Lust can also take you on a primrose route. Lust makes you forget your own benefit. Fear is inimical to your development and success. Victory over your own foibles is the victory over the world. A person in control of himself controls the world. Remove all your erroneous zones from your personality and find the comfort and you will be firmly ensconced on the throne of success.

55

Range from Eight to Eighty

Develop your personality to such an extent that you can mix up with any age group. This will keep you young and wise.

If you are comfortable with an eight-year-old child you will grow young mentally and will be cheerful. If you converse with an eighty-year-old you will earn a lot of wisdom. If you range from eight to eighty you will never be short of time.

You will learn new things from young people and the wisdom and experience from the old. You will be the most sought after person. Your repertoire of knowledge new, old and wisdom will be vast. If you mingle with all the age group you will always feel young and at the same time mature. You will become an erudite person without having to go through the grind. Be eager to learn from young and the old alike forever, your life will then be worthwhile.

Anecdote :

Former president of India, Abdul Kalam Azad enjoys the company of young and old alike. His penchant for the young is known to all of us. He has lots of hope from the young to make India a developed country at par with America. Jawaharlal Nehru was very fond of children and his birthday is celebrated as Children's Day.

56

Lend not More than What You can Afford to Lose

> Neither lender nor a borrower be – *William Shakespeare*

Lend not more than what you can afford to lose because when you lend to someone close to you if that person does not return the money you lose both the friend and the money. So make it your principle not to lend more than what you can afford to lose because you will be in a quandary.

You have no right to put your family in trouble. You will curse the day you lent the money. Lending money is as good as parting with some part of your life as earning money involves lot of efforts and pain. Standing guarantee to others is also fraught with danger. You must obtain counter-guarantee from that person. People are very humble and present a very grim picture while requesting for a loan and become ruthless and indifferent when you ask back the loan.

Anecdote

There are many examples for this. Look into the figures of NPAs of banks (Non-performing assets-NPA) and you will know how people renege on the promise to pay back the loan. Even the rich and well-to-do people resort to defaulting.

••

57

Every Human Being is Unique

A bad original is better than a good imitation

No two human beings are similar. Every human being is unique. Never imitate others and try to be different. Each individual has some distinct qualities which he needs to develop.

Never imitate others. You build a distinct identity of your own. Everyone must find his own destiny and purpose in life.

The world rewards uniqueness. In the beginning you may imitate and emulate a famous person but afterwards you must become a trail blazer in your own right. You must identify your own uniqueness and purpose. You are your own best judge. Try to understand yourself and act accordingly. If you imitate someone you may succeed for a while but then you will not get self-satisfaction.

Anecdote

Mahatama Gandhi, Amitab Bacchan, Sachin Tendulkar, Jack Welsh are few examples of uniqueness.

58

You are Born Everyday

> There is light at the end of the tunnel

Do not be overawed by the fact that with each passing day you are growing old. You are growing wiser if you make conscious effort to learn new things. You are as good as dead when you are asleep and when you wake up in the morning you are born again. Each sunrise is the harbinger of great opportunities waiting to be seized and exploited.

Treat every day as a new life. Don't worry about the past and future, focus only on the present. Present is the greatest gift you give to yourself. There is an old saying "Today is the first day of the rest of your life". However much you wish and desire bygone is bygone and no body can retrieve yesterday and lost time. Every morning brings new hopes and aspirations. Tell yourself everyday morning that it is a "wonderful day" and it will turn out to be wonderful. Accept the challenge thrown each day and you will grow stronger and you will have no regrets for growing old. Aging is not necessarily bad if you strive to excel and live life worthwhile.

Make new friends, learn new things, learn new skills and new words and that would keep you always young. Celebrate every day as your birthday and you will feel elated and full of exuberance.

Anecdote

Col Sanders of Kentucky Chickens started his business when he was well beyond sixties. Bob Simpson captained the second strung Australian team when Australia visited India. He not only scored a century at the age of 40 but also won the cliff-hanger series.

••

59

Prioritize Necessity, Comfort and Luxury

> You can satisfy your need but not your greed – *Mahatma Gandhi*

If you want to make both the ends meet and live a comfortable life prioritize your needs in the order of necessity, comfort and luxury.

First take care of the necessities and if you are left with resources then switch to comforts and then if you are still left with resources then spend on luxury. If you change the order then you will be in a financial fiasco. Decide your own agenda. However it would be better to give priority in the order of necessities, comforts, and luxuries.

Aspiring for luxury is not bad but squandering limited resources on luxuries is fraught with risk. Many people resort to cutting costs; on the contrary it is better to augment your income. Buying on credit cards is a very dangerous proposition since the rate of interest is very high and you are putting your future in dire straits. Only when you are sure about your future income it is advisable to use credit cards.

Anecdotes

There are many examples of people getting into debt trap. Debt trap is death trap. Very few people succeed in getting out of the quagmire of debt.

••

60

Walk Your Talk

> One who walks his talk is assured of success and honoured by all

Learn to walk your talk and you will enjoy the new-found confidence in yourself. If you talk a lot about your intentions to do things and do not carry out the commitment then you will be taken seriously by anyone and also yourself. Start with smaller commitments and march on to bigger things of walking your talk. Walking the talk is probably one of the toughest thing to do in the world but that should not limit your dreams. If you commit yourself to walking your talk that will give you lot of energy, enthusiasm and effervescence. Put yourself under pleasant pressure to walk what you talk. Hypnotise yourself into believing that you can achieve anything you set your sights on.

Anecdote

Bill Gates, Amitabh Bacchan, Late Dhirubhai Ambani all walked their talk inspite of doubting their capabilities. Your belief in yourself is vital to your success and not the opinions of other people. You are the best judge of yourself.

••

Enjoy Every Moment of Your Life

> Enjoy life as if today is the last day, as you never know whether you will see tomorrow's sunrise.

Enjoy every moment of your life whether at play, work or doing anything. You will never have any regrets if you enjoy every moment. Life is too brief for worrying, fretting, and brooding. If you fail to enjoy, then that moment is lost forever.

Life is too precious to be lost on trivial things. Extract pleasure from everything you do. Human life is the greatest gift of nature and should be fully exploited. Find enjoyment in every moment and you will relish life. If you curse and criticize you will continue wasting time. Some people's hobby is of picking holes in everything and they keep fuming and spoil their 's and other's life. Life is meant to be enjoyed and not for frivolous things like criticizing, fretting and worrying. If you enjoy every moment of your life then you will always feel young and agile.

Anecdote

Benjamin Franklin enjoyed every moment of life. Socrates enjoyed his philosophical quest every moment of his life.

62

Do your Best and Leave the Rest

> Hope for the best and prepare for the worst

Never settle for the second best in whatever you are doing as that would become your habit. Old habits die hard it is said. Always strive to do your best and leave the rest as high expectations may lead to frustration. Anything short of best will put you in doubt and you will never achieve your cherished goal. Doing your best will give you a lot of satisfaction even though you may fail. However in the long run you are bound to succeed. Doing your best will not give you any cause for regrets.

Anecdote

Freedom fighters of India like Jhansi Ki Rani, Netaji Subhash Chandra Bose, Veer Sawarkar, Bal Gangadhar Tilak and the host of others did their best and left the rest. Their contributions are no less than Mahatma Gandhi and the like.

••

63

Look at the Plus Points and Not at the Negatives

> While looking at the moon look not at its craters

It is human nature to look at the weak points of other people and resort to the slander game. Most of the time people engage in mud–slinging and disparaging others. If you look for good things in others you will find something to admire. Every person however villainous he may be has some good qualities.

To find a diamond one has to do a lot of cutting polishing and refining. Unless you go deep into the sea you cannot find pearls. The more you fathom into another person you will find a treasure trove of diamonds. That person will thank you for being a connoisseur and will be a great friend of yours.

Finding faults makes the other person defensive and he also resorts to criticism and your relations are soured. Always make it a point to look at the good things in others rather than focusing on their bad qualities. If you nourish good things with fertilizers then you will have a good crop and if you nourish bad things with fertilizer you will only grow weeds. Choice is entirely yours. The blame game is the worst sports inimical to salubrious relations. The more you admire good qualities the more it will thrive and the more rewarding and enriching it will be.

Anecdote

Andrew Carnegie the great American Steel magnate made good use of rewarding the right qualities and succeeded beyond imagination. He created a very congenial atmosphere in the factory where workers engaged themselves in healthy competition.

Even inveterate criminals have high opinion about themselves. Late V. Shantaram's Hindi film "Do Aankhen Bara Haath" was a very famous film in which Shantaram was an ideal jailor who reforms the hardened criminals.

••

64

Do not Make Your Mind a Storehouse of Garbage

> Your mind is your greatest asset in your quest
> for Knowledge, Wisdom and Success

Human mind is so precious that it needs to be handled dexterously. Don't let useless information into your mind as that would not allow your mind to work efficiently. Fill your mind with positive, healthy and serene thoughts. Clear the mind of all garbage of negative thoughts, ideas, negative emotions like fear, worry, hatred, jealousy and filthy thoughts.

Watch your words they become Thoughts,

Watch your thoughts they become Action

Watch your action they become your Destiny

You must have total control on what thoughts must enter your mind. Ban the entry of bad thoughts. Fill your mind with healthy thoughts. Each time a bad thought occurs deliberately fill your mind with positive thoughts.

Deeply analyze information and turn it into knowledge. Deeply analyze knowledge and turn it into wisdom. Regularly and assiduously remove garbage from your mind lest it becomes a haven for devil. Mind is like a race horse. It requires good breeding, nourishing and caring.

Your success in life is directly related to how you shape your mind. Remain unruffled even in the face adversity. Conscious mind is just a tip of the iceberg and subconscious mind is the hidden portion of iceberg. Faith in yourself, imagination, dream and goal if fed into subconscious mind it finds solutions to everyone of your dreams. Plant the idea in your subconscious mind, nourish with positive emotions and you can achieve anything you dream of.

Mind is like a genie it gifts you anything you earnestly desire provided you put in required efforts and sacrifice. You constantly guide your mind to think in the direction of your goal and the subconscious mind finds the answer. If you allow any garbage then it becomes morbid and your formidable enemy. The choice is entirely yours what orders you want to give it to your mind.

Mind is a warehouse capable of storing both garbage and diamonds. You must make a conscious effort to store the kind of commodity you want to store. Mind is a strong magnet as long as it stores pure things and loses its power if garbage is stored.

All the beautiful things in the world is the product of human mind. Human mind is such a wonderful thing that it is beyond words to portray it. Mind can make or mar your prospects depending upon how you use it. Mind is a very fragile item like a glass and needs to be handled with care. Limitation exists in your mind. Set the bird of mind free from the self-limiting cage of doubt, worry, hatred, jealousy to fly high.

Anecdote

Emulate the examples of Mahatma Gandhi, Dr. Nelson Mandela, Bill Gates, Kroc of MacDonald fame. They never allowed the mind to become a dustbin. There are umpteen number of examples of great people who focused on their goal in spite of all the criticism. A tree laden with fruits only becomes the target of stone-pelting.

••

65

Give Pension To Tension

Pay Attention not to take tension

Tension is probably the worst enemy of human beings playing havoc with mental, spiritual and physical health.

Tension clouds your vision and affects your problem-solving abilities. Keeping your cool in times of crisis helps the mind to think coolly and find a solution. In modern times tension is probably the number one killer. Tension generates lot of adrenaline juices and affects your health and also it puts a lot of pressure on your heart. Keep away tension and you will feel very much relaxed and ebullient.

Do away with tension from your repertoire of mental faculties and you will thank yourself profusely for the rewards are abounding. Let anything happen or let there be any adversity let not tension play havoc with your analytical mind. Make a commitment to yourself that you will remain unruffled and never allow tension to affect your judgement.

Anecdote

If you are asked to jump from an aeroplane with the help of a parachute and if you are a temperamental person you will probably not open the parachute. A cool mind is worth ten tense minds. Take the examples of fighter pilots. How cool they need to be as you never know when the enemy missile is going to hit the plane or there is some mechanical defect. You might have experienced yourself while driving a two-wheeler or a car how calm you have to remain in the midst of traffic.

••

66

ABCD of Success

Ambition, **B**oldness, **C**ommitment, **D**esire

A stands for ambition B stands for boldness C stands for commitment and D for desire (Strong Desire). You need to have all the four ingredients to succeed. If you have ambition, boldness, commitment and have no desire then the ambition will die a natural death. If you have ambition, boldness, desire but not commitment then the ambition will remain merely an ambition. If you have ambition, desire, commitment but lack boldness you will be frightful of taking any action. If you have boldness, commitment, desire and you lack ambition you will lose yourself in the way. Blending of all the attributes is necessary to achieve success.

Anecdote

Examples of people who might have used this formula are many: Andrew Carnegie, Bill Gates, Dhirubhai Ambani, Benjamin Franklin, Edison, Kroc of MacDonald fame.

Change Your Perception and Your World Changes

Your view of life makes the world look the way it looks. For eons the world has been like this. You see whatever you are looking for. If you look at the demeaning things then you will find the world bad. On the other hand if you look at the world with rosy glasses then you will find the world rosy. Your perception makes you look at the world the way you want to.

Change your perceptions and your world changes. Remove all the weeds of negativism from your mind and plant seeds of positive things. Your perception is negative if you keep complaining about everything including weather, people and things.Your psyche will become like that. You must emulate those people who looked at the world with positive mind.

Anecdote

Abraham Lincoln always looked at his problems with a positive frame of mind. His perceptions were positive. Any other person with distorted perception would have given up. But inspite of many failures he grew from the ashes like Phoenix. Our own Late Dhirubhai Ambani could have remained poor but his perception about self and the world was optimistic.

••

Be Childlike and Not Childish

However much you grow old but remain always a child at heart. Childlike innocence, smile and unbiased countenance are virtues one must cultivate. Being childlike has many advantages as people look at you with sympathy and admiration. On the other hand childishness is equivalent to being a stubborn mule. You will always want to have everything your way without consideration for others. Childishness is being adamant without listening to logic and love. A childish person will fight for frivolous things and for him he is the whole world. Childishness tantamount to immaturity. Childish person will always be obsessed with his own thinking without listening to others.

Anecdote

Jawaharlal Nehru was very fond of children and because of his childlike attitude he was near and dear to everyone. His birthday is celebrated as Children's Day. Our former President of India Abdul Kalam Azad also has a childlike personality. He mingles with children easily and is very comfortable with them.

••

69

Men are Men and Women are Women

It is foolish to be different than one's natural gender.

Men are physically stronger are logical and less loquacious compared to women. Women are more gentle, graceful, garrulous, and loving. Of late career women try to be masculine leaving their home turf. Women are better off in their feminine grace. Nature has made both in different moulds. Let women compete with men in every field but certainly should not leave their feminity. Women are very different from men in every respect. Without women this world would have been bereft of the most beautiful creation of nature. Men should also not emulate and compete with women in the feminine field. Both have distinct identity and should be maintained.

Anecdote

Indira Gandhi and Margaret Thatcher ruled their respective countries with iron hand but maintained their feminine grace. Kiran Bedi the famous police officer is a classic example of toughness and feminine grace.

To conclude, you must count your blessings without cursing your fate or position in your life. You can almost achieve

anything in life provided you have a strong will and are ready to make full use of all your resources. Give your best to the society and you will get back thousand times more returns.

Aspire to make your life worthwhile as human life is more precious than all the wealth of the world put together. Never ever fritter away your time in useless pursuits like fear, jealousy, worry, gossiping and criticizing but focus your full attention to fulfill your purpose in life. Every human being is unique and can contribute tremendously to society. Listen to your conscience and carry on your mission with passion and live life worthwhile.

••

70

Develop Forgiveness

To err is humane to forgive is divine

Forgiveness is a quality which will bring harmony, peace and solace to your self.

Unless we forgive we will always carry the emotional baggage on our mind. Forgiveness requires lot of courage and resolve. Only the strong can forgive. If you do not forgive the resentment will keep lingering in your mind and torment you to no end. Forgiveness will relieve you from resentment and turmoil.

Forgiving yourself is also vital as you may nurse relentless guilt gnawing your conscience. Forgiveness is akin to divinity. Developing this quality will always keep you happy and blissful. Forgiving others may be a boon as it may create enmity and all the while you will be thinking about that person. Forgiveness makes the other person totally relaxed and becomes a great friend of yours.

Anecdote

Priyanka Wadhera daughter of Late Rajiv Gandhi forgave the assassins of her father thus giving relief to the assassins as well as herself. There are plethora of examples in human history of forgiveness. Gautam Buddha forgave the assassin who tried to assault him thus setting a great precedent and manifesting supreme courage and grace.

Morality is the order of the day, but the pristine glory of morality will continue to sustain.

••